THE DOGHOUSE

JAN THOMAS

Houghton Mifflin Harcourt

Boston   New York

For Peter

www.hmhco.com

The illustrations in this book were done digitally.

ISBN: 978-0-544-85003-3

Manufactured in China
SCP 10 9 8 7 6 5 4 3 2 1
4500700829

Oh no! The ball went into **THE DOGHOUSE.**

Who will get it out?

So Cow goes into
THE DOGHOUSE.

But Cow does not come out.

Now Cow AND the ball are
in **THE DOGHOUSE**.
Who will get them out?

So Pig goes into
THE DOGHOUSE.

But Pig does not
come out.

QUACK
QUACK

Now Cow and Pig
AND the ball are in
THE DOGHOUSE.
Who will get them out?

So Duck goes into
THE DOGHOUSE.

But Duck does not come out.

Can you come out, Duck?

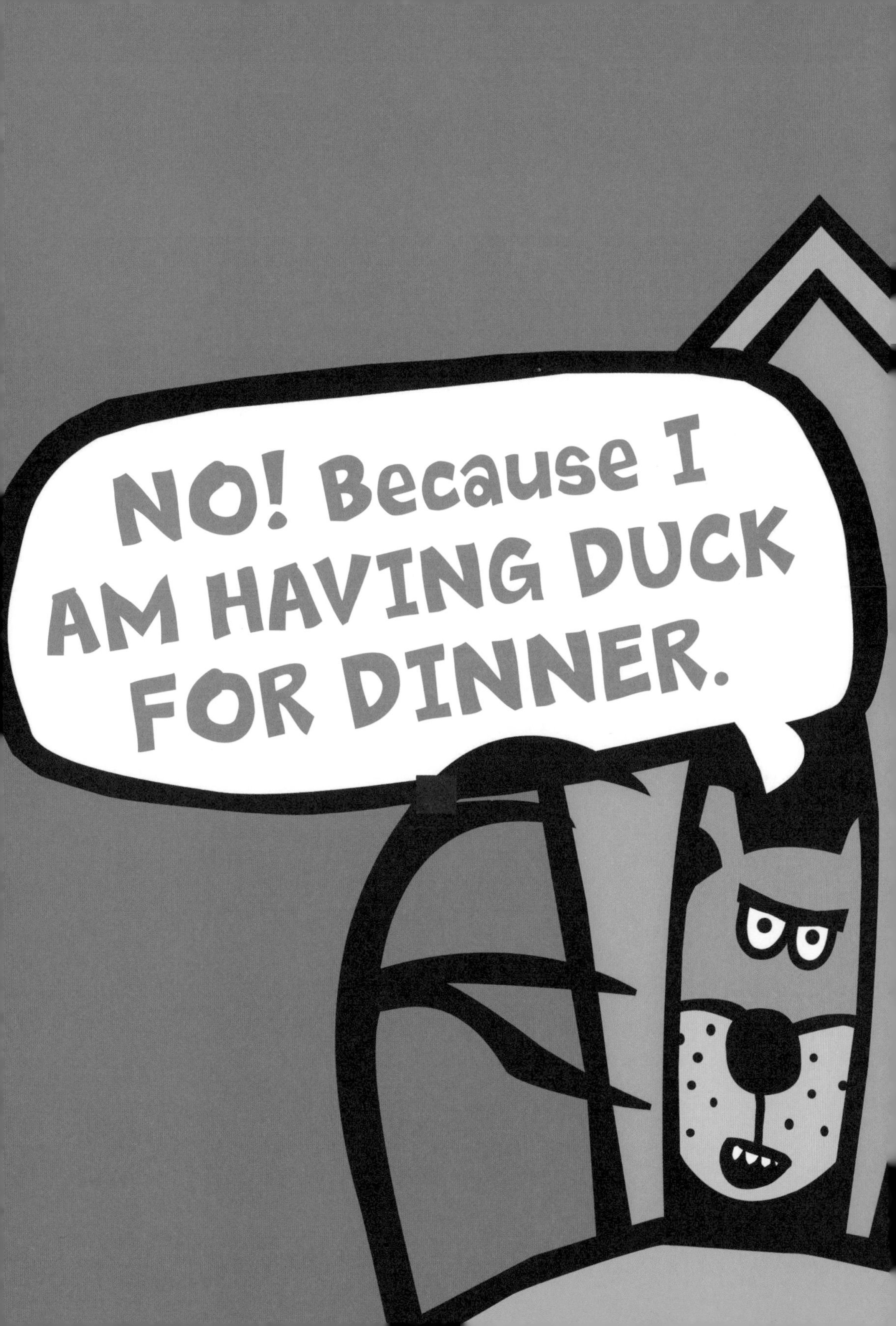
NO! Because I AM HAVING DUCK FOR DINNER.

Get your child ready to read in three simple steps!

1 **I READ**	Read the book to your child.
2 **WE READ**	Read the book together.
3 **YOU READ**	Encourage your child to read the book over and over again.

Looking for more laughs?

Don't miss these other adventures
from Jan Thomas: